MW01043477

To everyone who has ever loved an animal with their whole heart,
you are my kind of people!

"Surround yourself with animals and people who are kind to them."
–Anonymous

MASCOT BOOKS

**www.mascotbooks.com**

***The Cat Named Ron***



**For more information, please contact:**
Mascot Books
620 Herndon Parkway, Suite 320
Herndon, VA 20170
info@mascotbooks.com

Library of Congress Control Number: 2019903736

CPSIA Code: PRT0719A
ISBN-13: 978-1-64307-573-0

Printed in the United States

Author photos by T.R. Armstrong Photography

Aubrey-
Hugs & Kitties!
Kelly Jean Lietaert

KELLY JEAN LIETAERT

Hi there! My name is Ron. I'm a tabby cat, which is one of the most common breeds of cats. But...I would like to think that I'm not just any ordinary cat. I have many fun and different qualities that I'd like to share. First of all: how many other cats do you know that could write a book? While you think about that, I'll share with you how I met my forever family.

I was born at the Humane Society. All day long, I stayed in a cage with a few other kittens. We were tiny then, so there was plenty of room. They named me "Tiger," but I just knew that once I had a family, my name would change. I was very active. Most of the other kittens just wanted to sleep all the time, but not me! One day, a family came in looking for a new pet. They asked if I could be released from my cage so they could play with me. I won their hearts instantly and they decided to take me home with them! I was super excited, and the other kittens looked happy to see me go, too.

Just making sure my pen works!

Me

When I arrived at my forever home, there were so many new things to see. But first, my family showed me where the litter box was. I guess that was important. I couldn't wait to show them that I already knew how to use it by myself! Next, they took me into a big room that they called a "kitchen" and showed me two bowls that had food and water in them. I knew right away that this spot was going to be one of my favorites!

Best Buddies

After that, they introduced me to my furry sister, Mocha. Sadly, she wasn't very happy to meet me. In fact, she hissed and growled at me, which scared me a little, since I was just a baby. She later told me she was upset that her family had gotten another cat, because she thought she would get less attention. That wasn't true at all, and now we are very good friends...except when I run and jump on her, which is what I thought little brothers were supposed to do.

Mocha's contribution

The softer the blanket, the longer the nap.

Back then I was so tiny that I needed help getting up on the bed. That night, I chose to sleep with one of my sisters. Nowadays, I sleep with everyone! I try to change beds every night because I don't want any of my family to be sad. I hear them telling each other that I "hog the bed," but I think that means they love it when I sleep right in the middle and stretch out as much as possible. I especially love super-soft blankets. I rub my face in them and they remind me of my cat mom.

Looking outside is one of my favorite things to do!

I have grown a lot since I was adopted. Back then, I was small enough to be held in the palm of someone's hand. But now I'm a big boy, and I sometimes forget how big I am. I especially love to sit on the end table and look out the windows. Sometimes, I knock things off of the table if I see a bird, chipmunk, or squirrel—that's when I get a little crazy! It's a good thing I'm so cute...at least that's what my mom tells me every day.

I am also very curious. I sniff everything, and am sometimes more like a dog than a cat. Every morning when my mom is waking my sisters up, I smell everything in their room, just to make sure it's all the same as the night before. I also have other important jobs, such as leading them down the stairs in the morning, which typically ends with them tripping over me and saying my name very loudly.

The best view of the kitchen is from the top of the fridge.

Helping with the laundry can be tough, but I always do my part!

That's not the only time I hear my family talking about me. Often, they wonder what I do with myself all day. Are they serious?! I am such a busy cat! I love to play with my puff balls, chase Mocha around, and jump on the refrigerator and pretend like I'm on top of a mountain. Later, I look out the windows, take a bath in the sunlight, sleep in the laundry basket, sleep on the couch, and sleep on each of the beds. Finally, I eat, then sleep on the floor by the fire. What else could I possibly be doing?!

I also try to be the best cat I can be. I love my family and I am so grateful for the love they give me. I let them do things to me like dress me in sweaters and make me "dance." I feel a little silly doing these things, but I know it makes them happy. They love to take my picture, too, which I always allow. I often look right at the camera, but sometimes I turn my head so they can see how cute the side of my face is, too.

I am a master of strategy...

...a good listener...

...and a snazzy dresser...

...sometimes!

A couple of practice naps.

I have mentioned several times that I love to nap, which is probably because I am a very good napper. I have several "go-to" positions when I am feeling sleepy. I am a pretty big boy, so sometimes I like to show off a little bit and make my body as long as I can. This position requires me to have the entire couch or bed to myself. Then other times, I like to curl up as tight as possible. In this position I look like a fur pillow, and you can't tell where I start and where I end. See?

I told you I was good at this! It takes a lot of practice to be a good napper, but I'm willing to put in the hours every day to perfect my techniques. I'm dedicated to being the best napper in the house, but Mocha has similar goals.

There's my forehead "M."

I bet you are wondering how I got the name Ron. I have to say, Ron is more of a nickname. It's a very long story, like most are when it comes to explaining how a nickname came to be. My official name is Max. I am a tabby cat and have an "M" on my forehead, so they wanted to name me something that started with an "M." But soon my humans were calling me all kinds of crazy things, and I responded to all names because I was hoping to get love or treats. I'm smart like that! One of my nicknames was the name Ron, and it just stuck. I like it and I think it suits me well.

~~Brian~~
~~Whiskers~~
~~Mittens~~
~~Tiger~~
Max
Ron

A wise cat once said:
"The grass is always greener
when you're with your family."

I am an indoor cat, which means I don't go outside by myself. But deep in my heart, I know I am wild. I sit by the door and cry, hoping someone will open it and I can sneak out. This convinced my family to let me explore outside for a little bit. My human mom was nervous that I may run away. I mean, really Mom. Why would I run away? I love my family! So, they ended up putting me on a leash and letting me walk around the backyard like that. I felt so silly, and I think I even heard the squirrels laughing at me.

After a few weeks, my mom let me walk around outside without the leash. I really love walking on our patio and sitting on the outdoor cushioned furniture. Sometimes, when I'm feeling brave, I walk all the way to the edge of the yard. I crouch down low when birds fly overhead. A few times when I first started going outside, I walked around to the front of the house and surprised my family by crying to be let in at the front door. They were amazed by my courage, and now agree that I am, indeed, a little bit wild.

Empty boxes
are my
favorite boxes.

I would have to say that Christmas is my favorite holiday. My family puts up a HUGE TREE in our living room, and I sit under it every day it's there. Mocha and I often wonder if there are velvet blankets under trees in the wild. We hope so. When my family decorates for Christmas, I have two very important jobs: first, I climb all the way up to the top of the ladder every year to make sure it's safe before they stand on it to decorate the tree. Next, I sit in all of the boxes as they are emptied of the decorations. It's fun for me, and I know my family appreciates my cuteness. I have many responsibilities, and I am happy to help in any way that I can.

Is dinner ready yet?

I really love to hang out in the kitchen. With six people and two cats in my family, there's always a chance at least one of us is standing by the counter. I especially love to sit on a stool at the island while my mom is preparing dinner. It's just the right height for me to be able to see what's going on, and maybe, just maybe, get a tiny taste of something yummy. Because let's be honest, it gets a little boring eating cat food all the time.

When my dad is traveling for work, I often sit in his chair at the table and visit with my family while they eat. I have very good manners and never beg. I just sit very politely and listen to my family talk about their day.

Hanging out
with Mocha!

Mocha and I have a lot of fun together. We both like to sniff things outside on the patio, run around the house as fast as we can at two in the morning, give each other baths, look out the window for birds and other creatures, and beg for treats when we see any of our family members in the pantry. But napping together is my favorite, because she is a very good cuddler.

happy
WINTER
days

I know I have an amazing life. My food bowl is always full, and if I can ever see the bottom of it, I just cry and my mom gives me more. I always have someone to snuggle with, and warm, soft blankets are always easy to find. My family picks me up and loves me all day long, and my furry sister is usually up for some fun – or a nap, which I enjoy just as much. Thank you for listening to my story. I hope you can hug a cat today...or a dog, they're not so bad, either!

THE END

## Word Scramble

| | | | |
|---|---|---|---|
| TCA | ________________ | OODF | ________________ |
| NRO | ________________ | PSNA | ________________ |
| FLIYMA | ________________ | UDTIESO | ________________ |
| EMHUNA ICSTYOE | ________________ | WLID | ________________ |
| OVLE | ________________ | CAMOH | ________________ |

## Discussion Questions

1. Ron was adopted from the Humane Society. Do you have a pet? From where did you get your pet?

2. Ron mentions that the kitchen is his favorite room in the house. What is your favorite room and why?

3. Ron loves to look out windows, take naps, and chase Mocha. What do you like to do?

4. Ron is actually a nickname – his real name is Max! Do you have a nickname? How did you get it, and do you like it?

5. Ron loves going outside where he enjoys sitting on the patio furniture, sniffing the plants, and running in the grass. What do you do when you're outside?

6. Ron and Mocha are best friends. They like to do things together. Who is your best friend and what do you like to do with him/her?

# Word Search

E H M Z F O A F T J

L N T S A A M I M R

Z R Z I M O C H A O

R X W K I T C H E N

Y K D M L H E V U X

L O V E Y F O O D D

C H R I S T M A S N

K F Y G Y J X E L A

W I L D H H E B P P

J H D Z V C A T S S

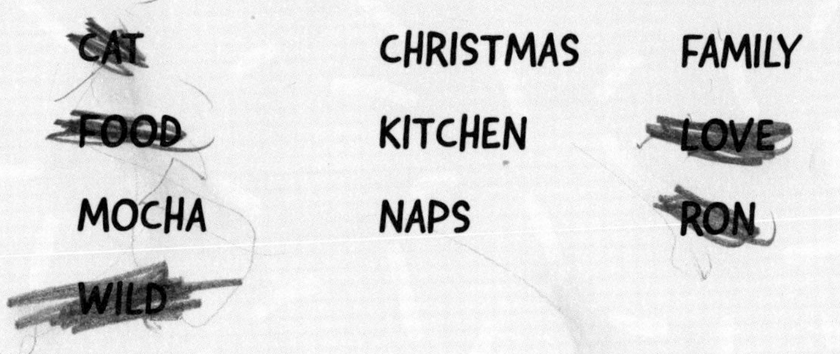

# About the Author

Ron is an 8-year-old tabby cat who is excited about his first book. Loved by everyone who meets him, his fur is soft and his purr is loud. He enjoys watching out the windows for chipmunks, napping on the couch, and meowing loudly while everyone in the house is trying to sleep.